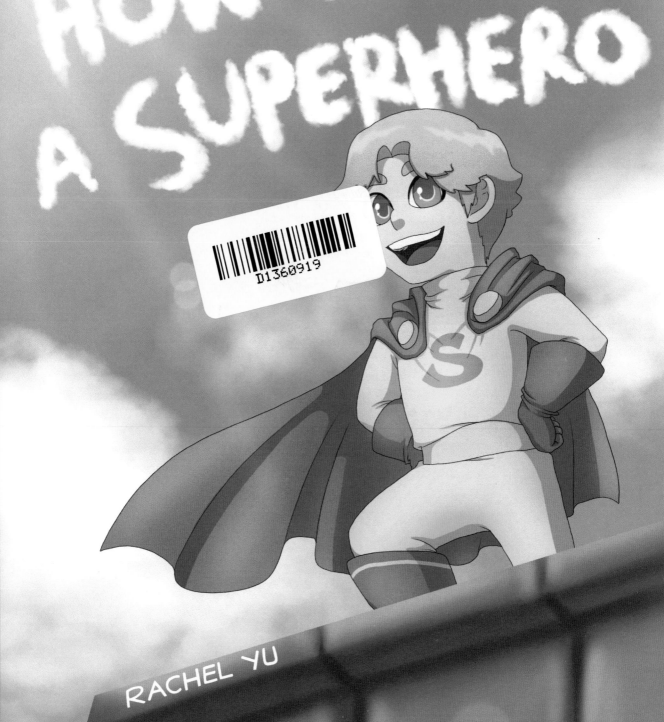

HOW TO BE A SUPERHERO

D1360919

RACHEL YU

www.rachelbookcorner.com

ISBN-10: 1468103008
ISBN-13: 978-1468103007

Printed in the United States of America.

For Mom, Dad, Eric, and Bear

"Greetings, citizen! I am...*drum roll*...Superior Guy! Yes, it is I, Superior Guy, the superhero of the century, and you, lucky citizen, will get to learn just how to be a spectacular superhero like me! (Well, almost as spectacular as me. After all, no one can out dazzle Superior Guy!)"

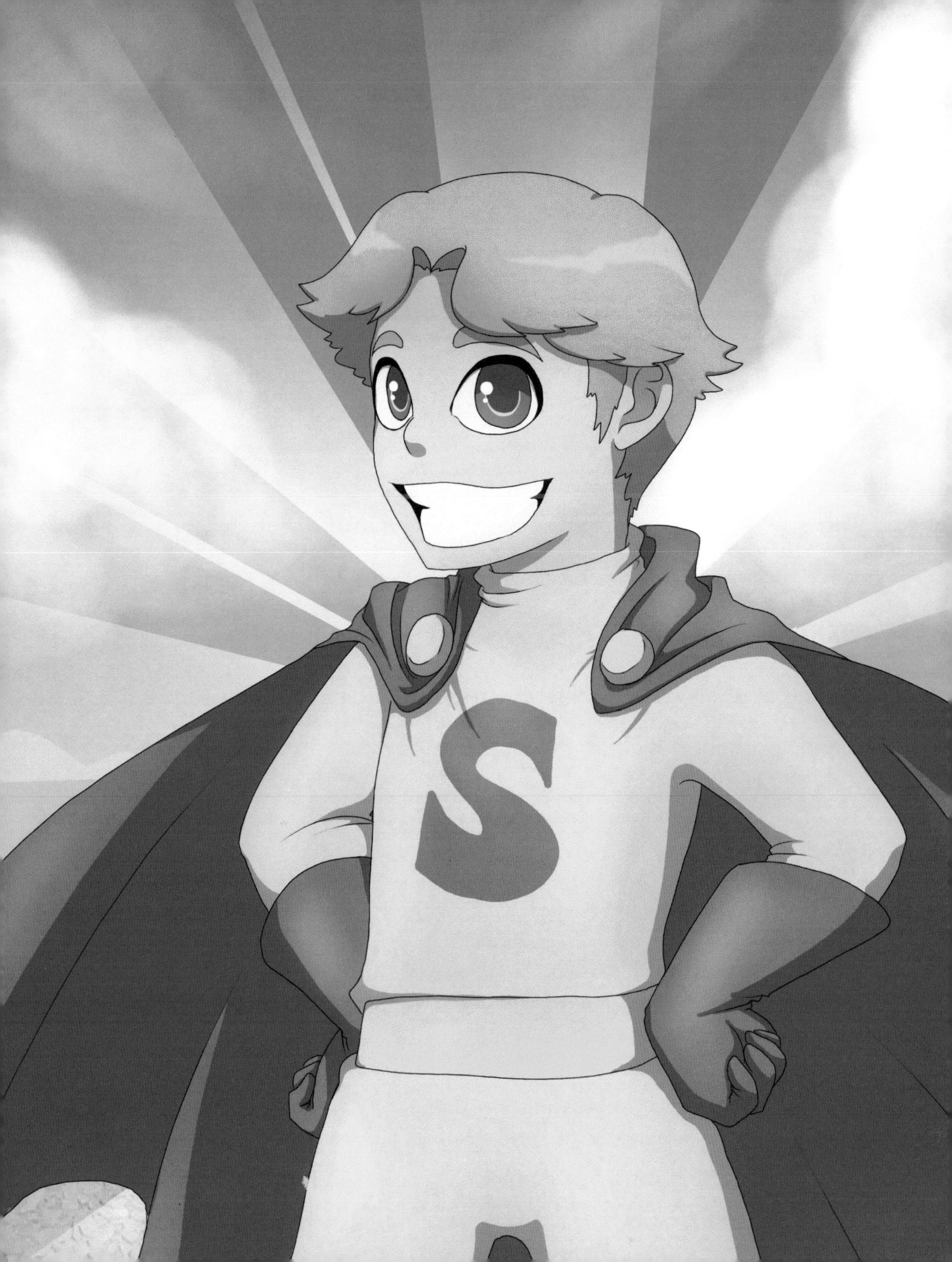

"Ahem. Here we are at my Castle of Brilliance, my home away from home, my fort of peace and quiet, which is safely hidden away in the Sahara Desert. Isn't it a magnificent looking place?

"Please wipe your shoes on the mat (I just had the floors waxed) and then we can get started on what makes a superhero."

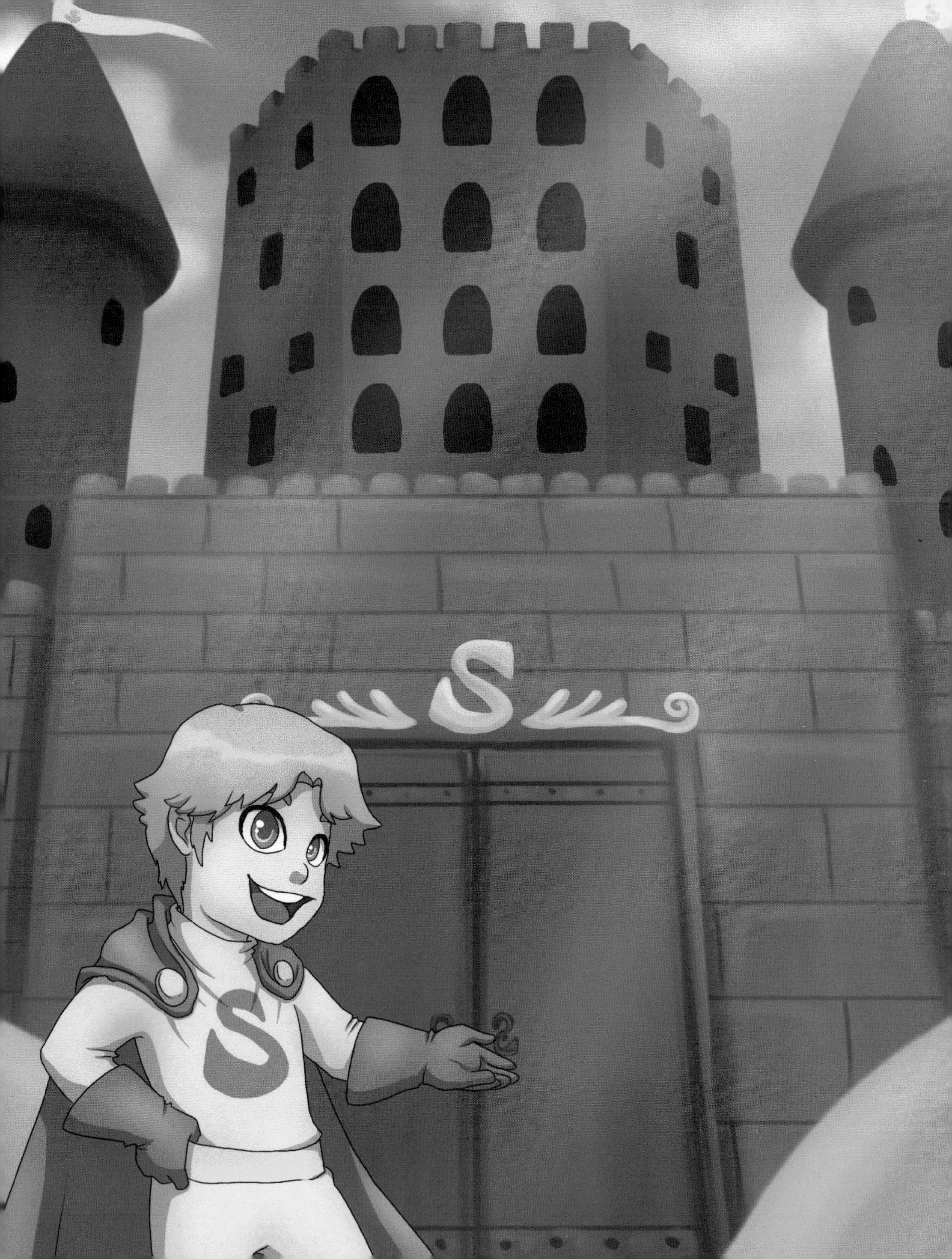

"To be a superhero, one must first have a secret origin. A secret origin is the story of how you received your powers and became a superhero.

"Some superheroes, for instance, are the result of bizarre, mad science experiments, while others simply fall into vats of toxic waste. The Human Light Bulb, for instance, got his illuminating powers after being exposed to Beta-Omega Radiation at the dentist's office.

"Other heroes are bestowed super abilities from mystical races, control magical instruments, or are actually aliens from another planet, like the Solar Sorceress who is native to Saturn."

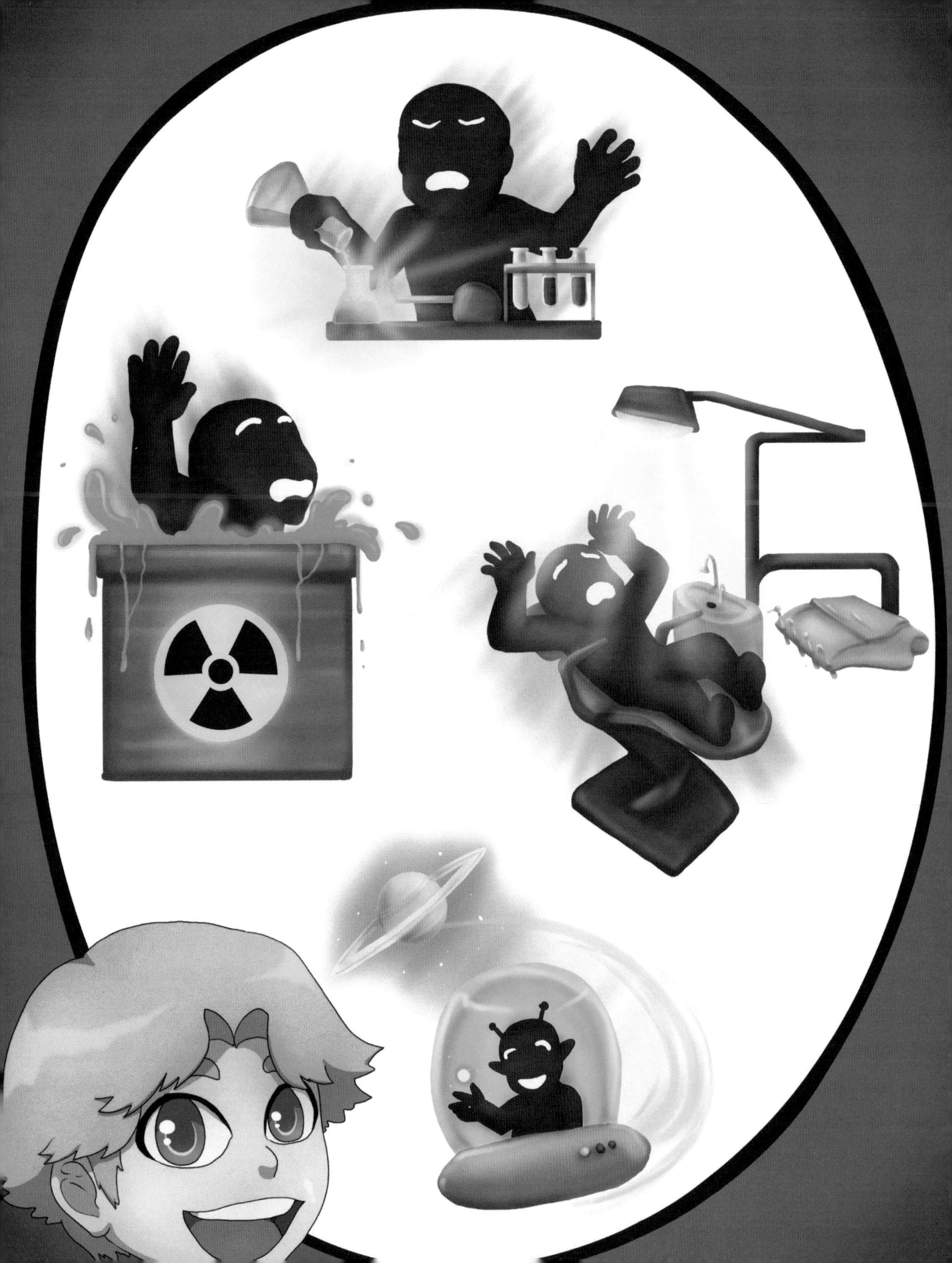

"These origins can result in different forms of power, such as telepathy, weather control, heat vision, and teleportation. The superhero, the Zipper, is gifted with super speed, while the heroine Madame Sparks can generate lightning. I myself possess super strength and flight, while also being able to shoot freeze rays from my eyes!"

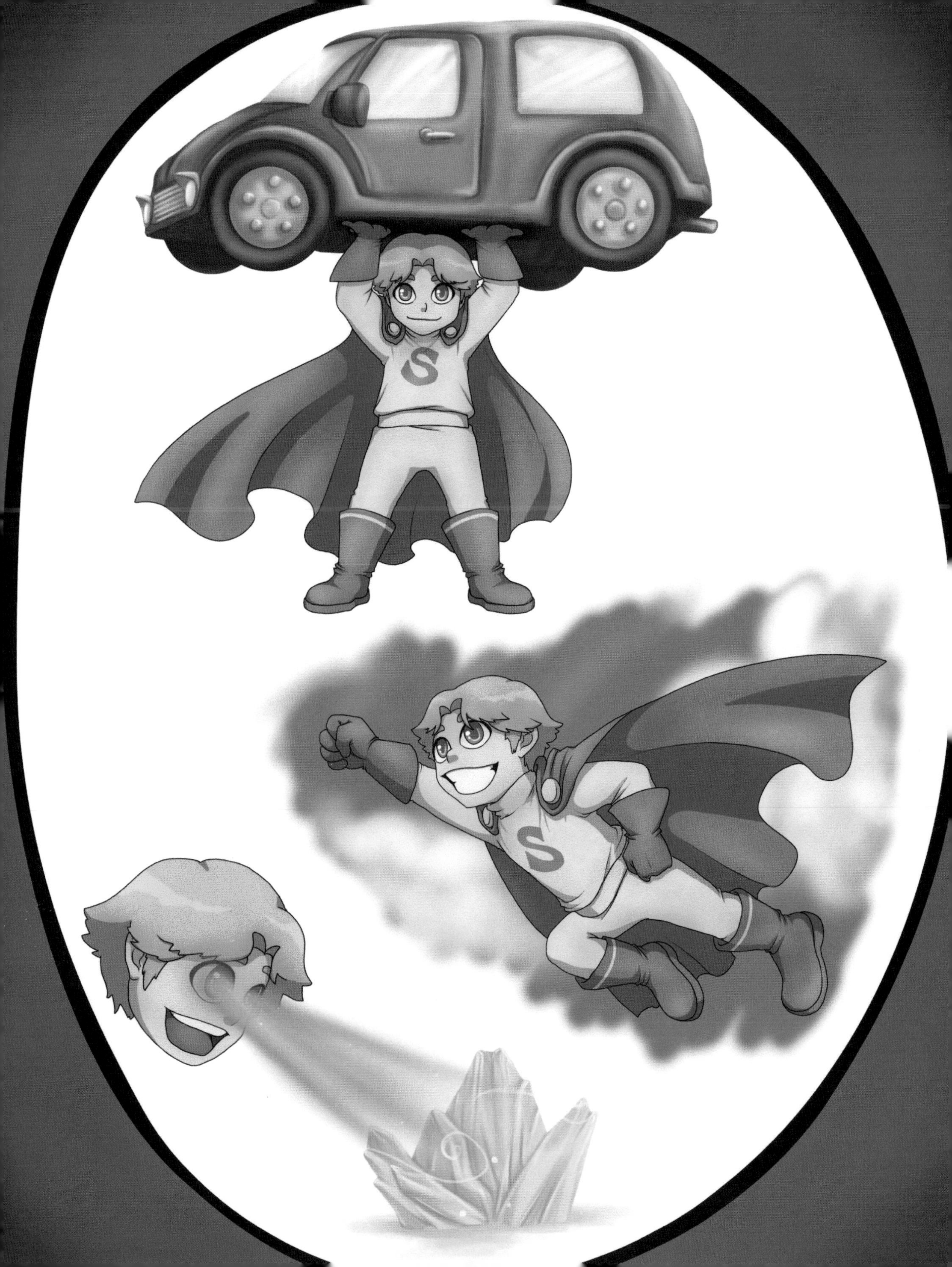

"However, some superheroes don't even have super powers. Certain colleagues of mine are ordinary humans who use their intellect, courage and advanced technology to battle evil. The Aluminum Man is one such earthling."

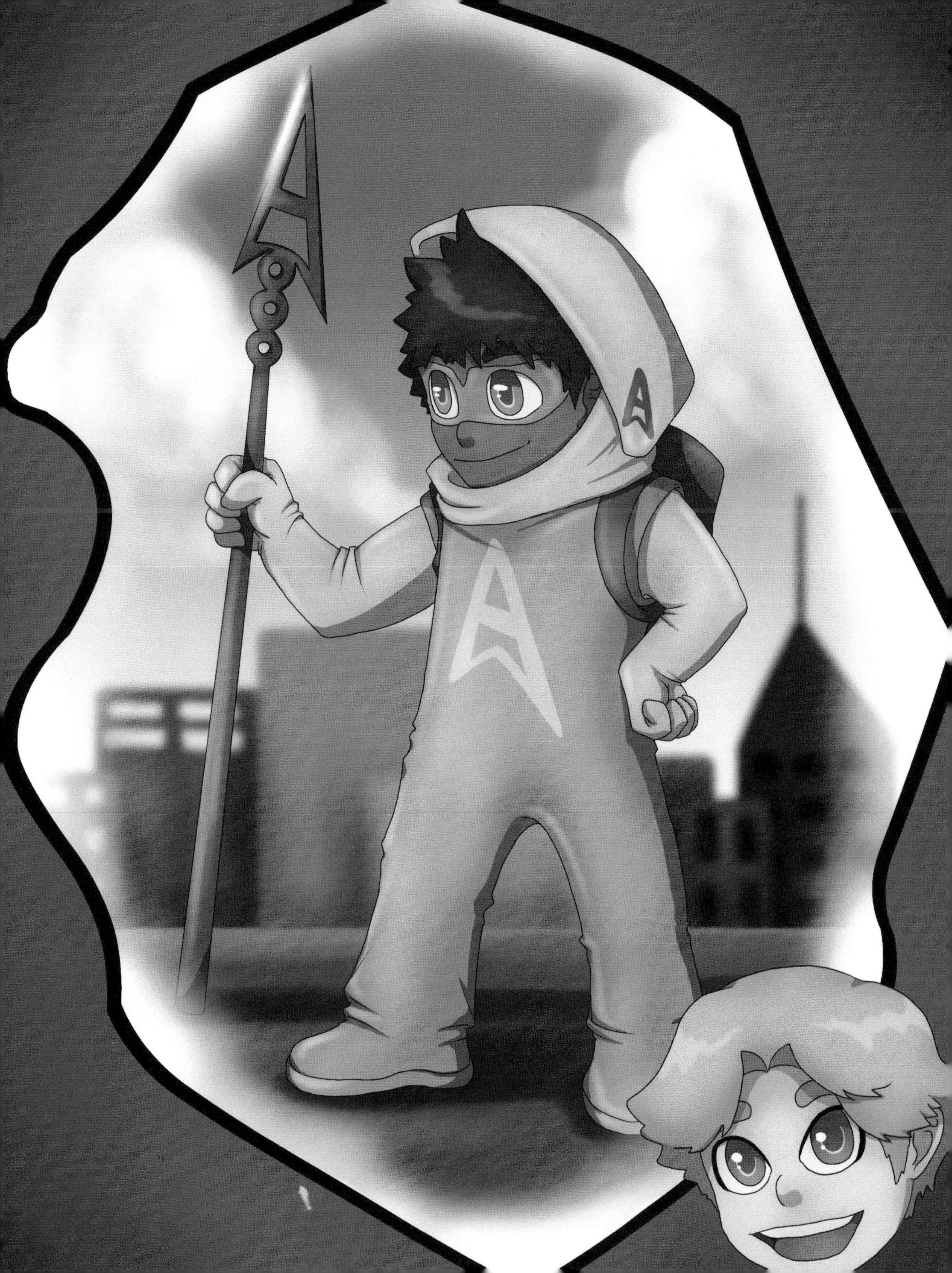

"Once you have your powers or super technology, you must master a very important ability. You must be able to pose. After all, a slouchy, duck footed, bowlegged, caped crusader isn't very appealing!

"Always look good in the public eye; you never know when your picture may appear on the front page. Remember to have a costume with bright, vibrant colors, so that photographers will be able to spot you easily. A long, billowing cape can help."

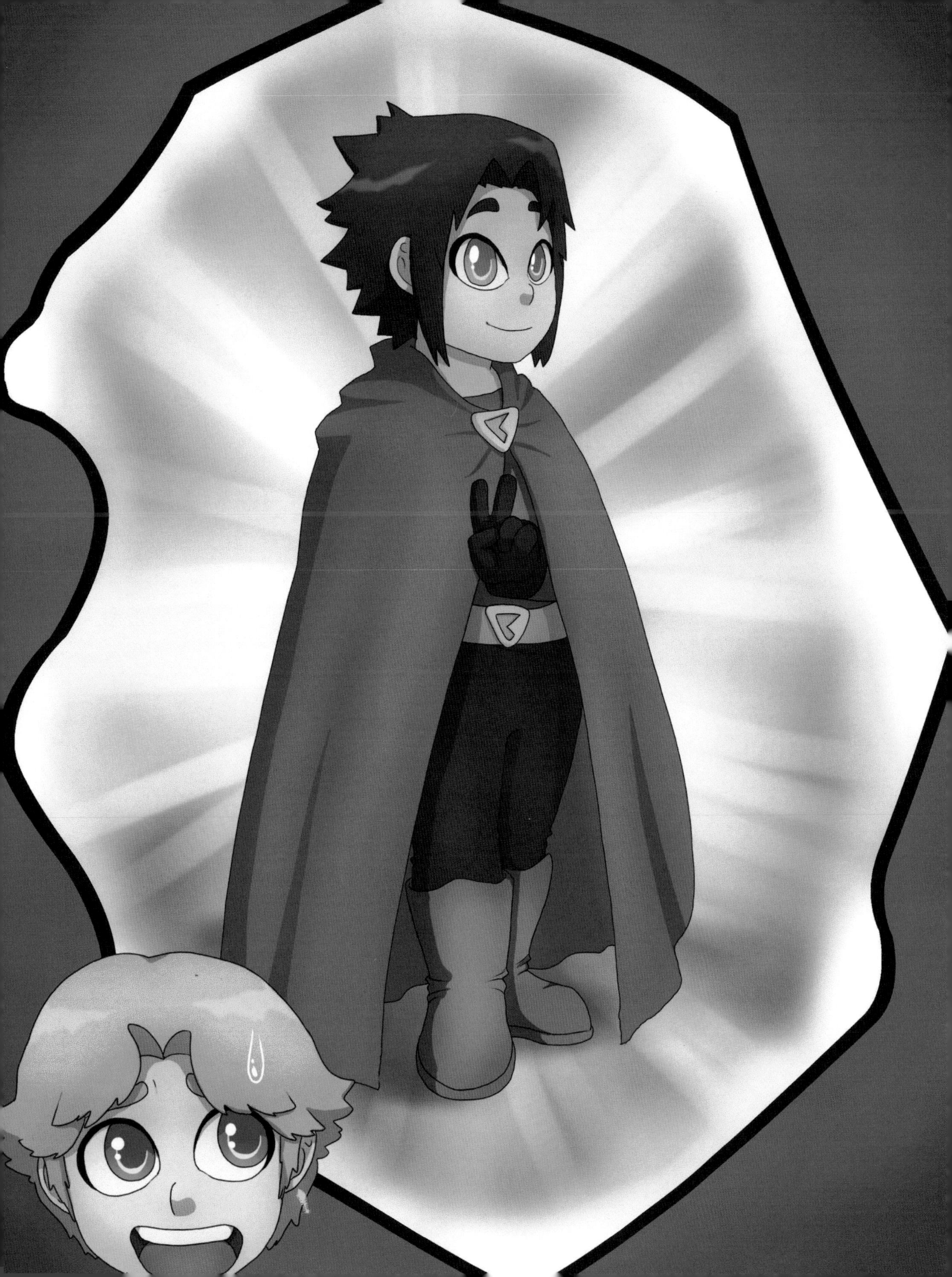

"When posing, puff out your chest and stare straight into the horizon. A raised fist or hands on the hip give a good sense of power and purpose. Note, a solid smile will do wonders, but first make sure you have nothing stuck between your teeth!"

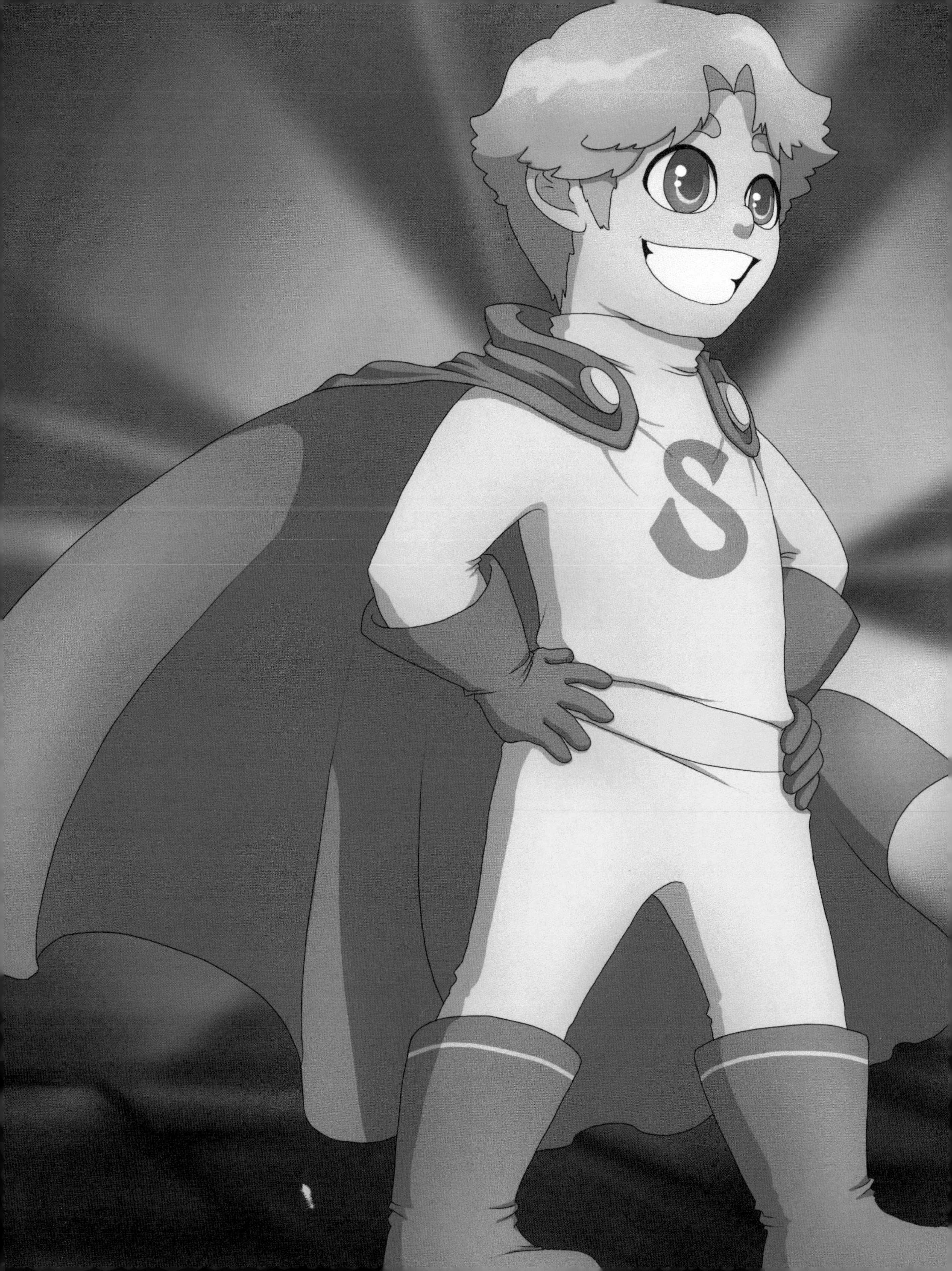
S

"Also, a catchphrase is a great thing to have when going into battle. Just before you have to fight the Insidious Squidmaster, pose and yell out your catchphrase. Something like "Kablam!", "Justice shall be dished!", or "Freedom Clubbers, Commence!" will do. My own personal one is "For Liberty, Duty, and Democracy!"

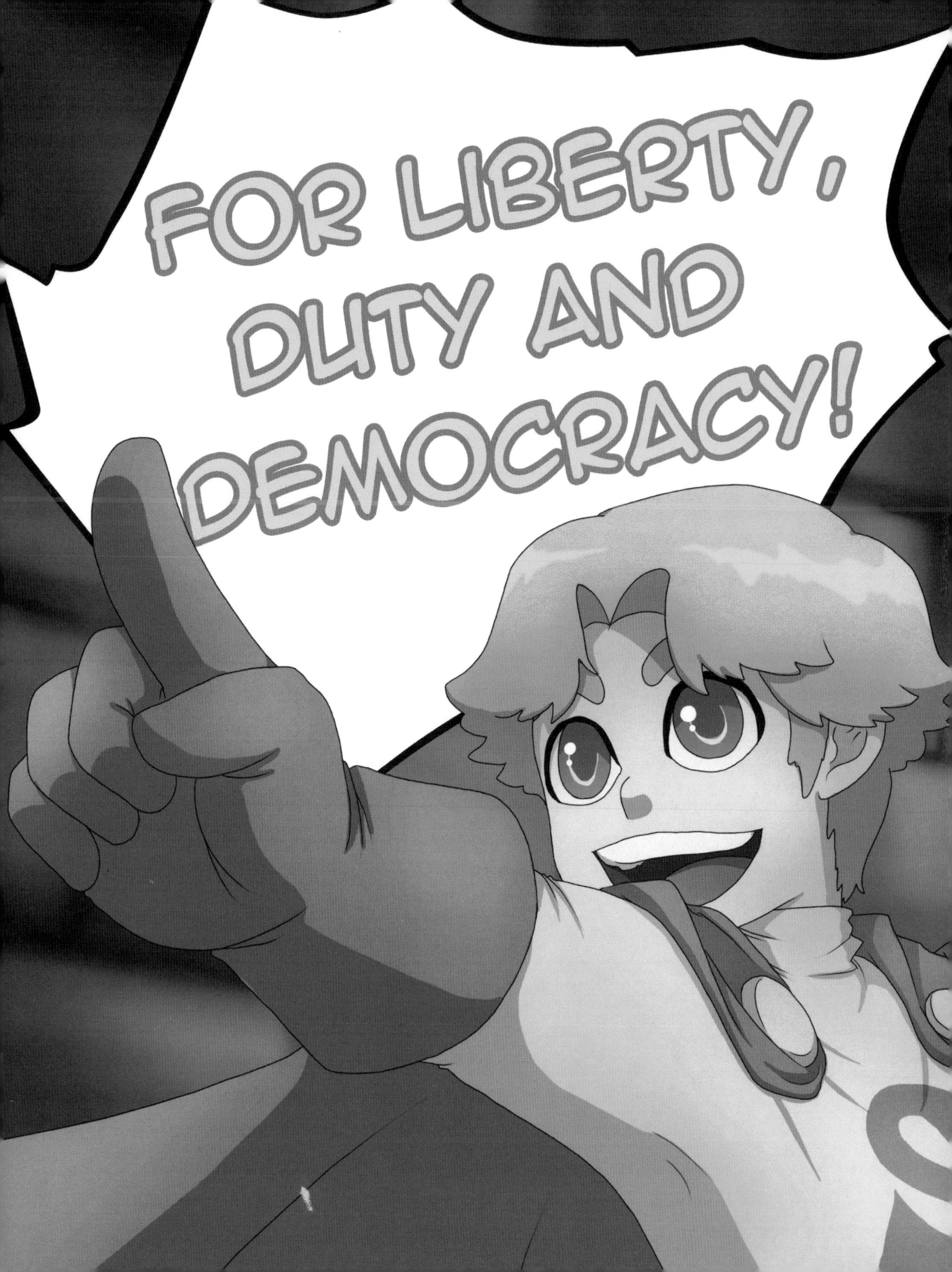
FOR LIBERTY, DUTY AND DEMOCRACY!

"In addition, you must be able to deal with the hordes of fans that will throw themselves at your feet, begging for your attention. To deal with them, you need an outstanding signature. It is a good idea to learn cursive. Make sure to flourish your letters, while moving your hand so as not to smear the ink. It's always a good idea to have a sharpie on hand."

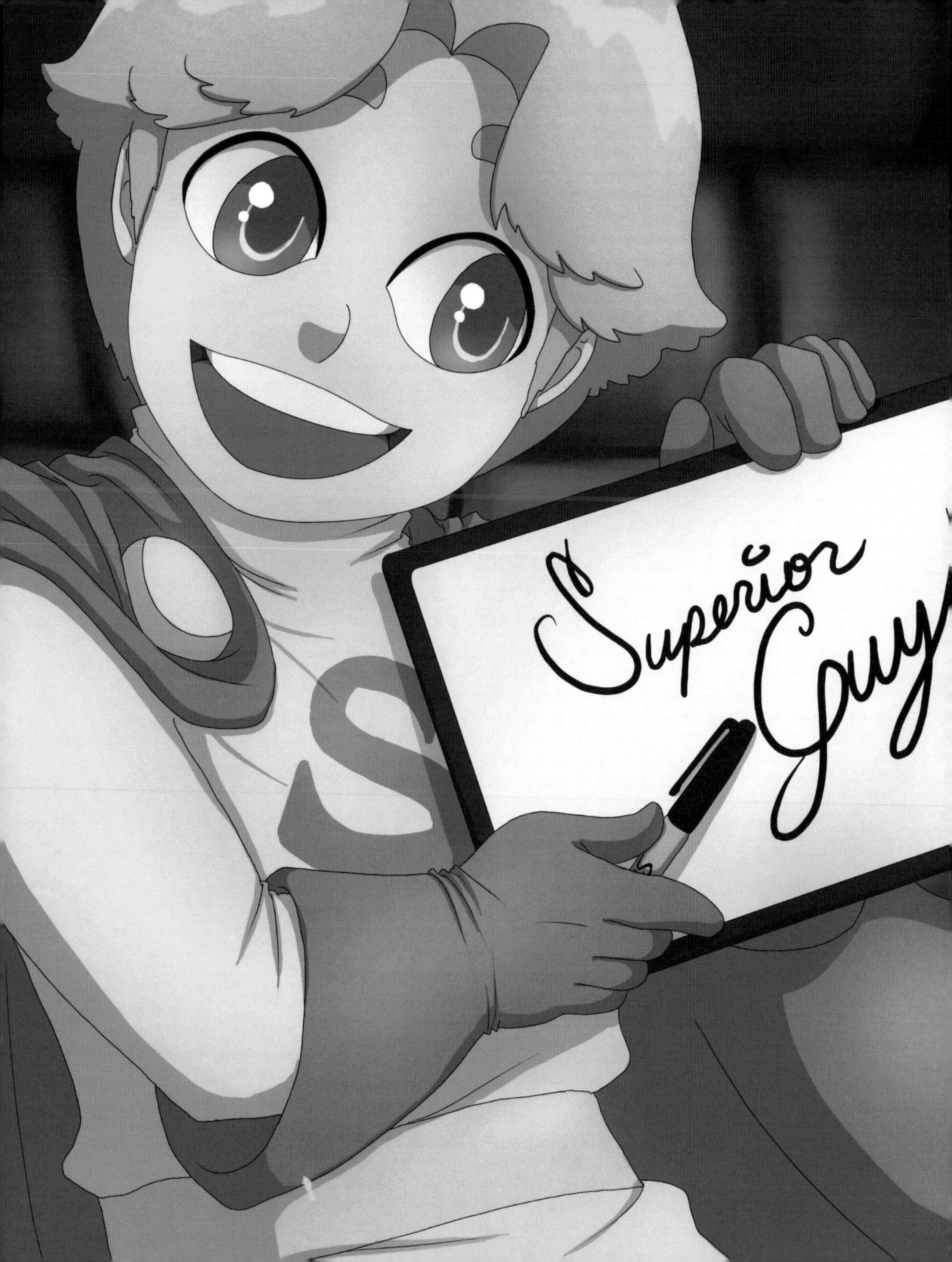
Superior
Guy

"While it is nice to be adored by the public, there are times when even an A-list superhero needs a break. A secret identity will give you the privacy you need.

"One way to create a secret identity is to wear a mask with your superhero costume. I do not do this; why should I cover up my glorious face? So, instead of wearing a mask, you can hide your civilian identity by wearing glasses, combing your hair differently, or adding a fake mustache!"

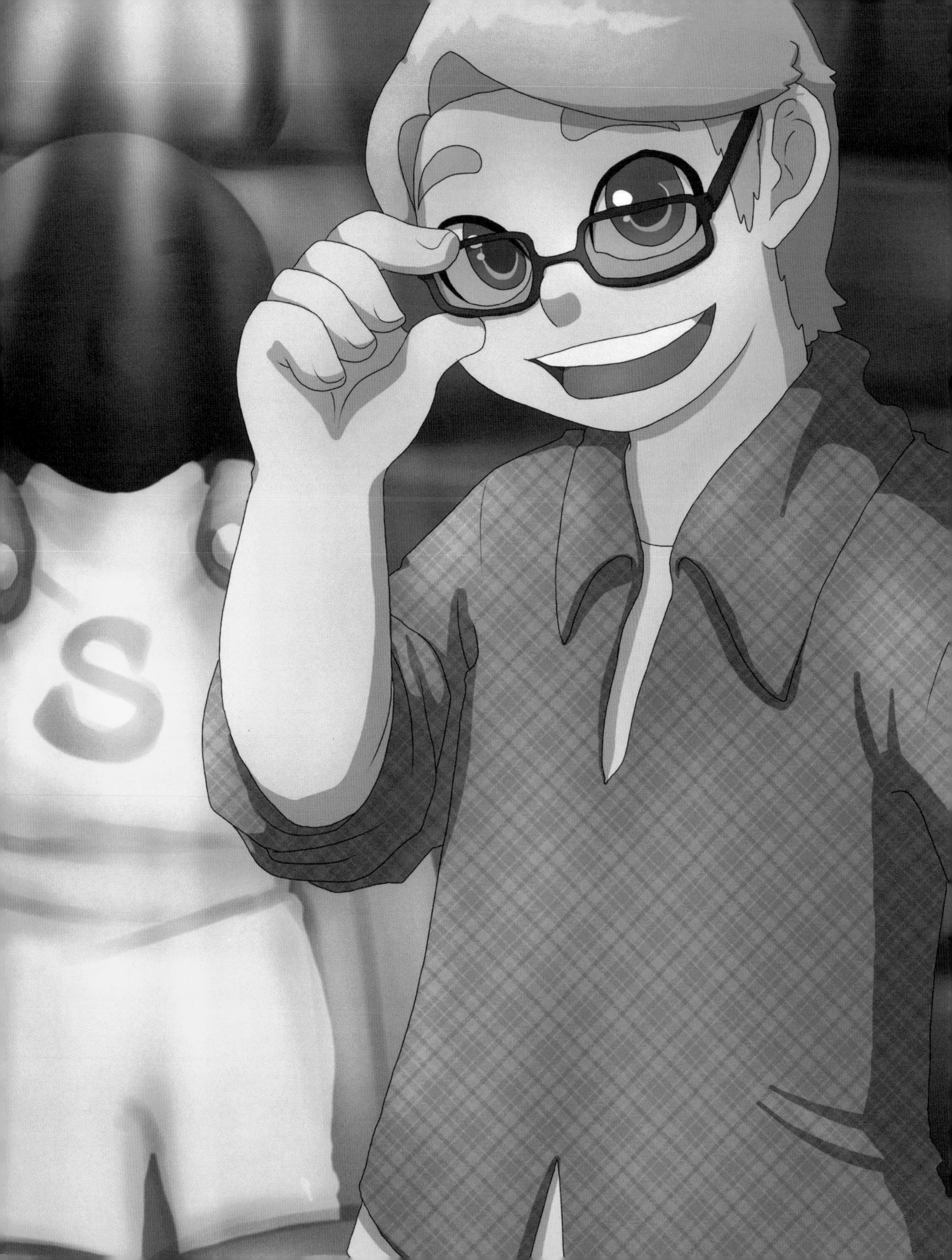
S

"Now, as a Superhero, you may want to invest in a sidekick. A sidekick is someone smaller, younger, and less spectacular than you. They are there to assist you in times of need, such as when your dry-cleaning needs to be picked up, or when your tux needs to be ironed, or when you need someone to wax the Superior-mobile. Do not get your sidekick confused with your dog, as a dog will tend to shed on your black dress coat (yes, Superior Dog, I'm talking about you!)."

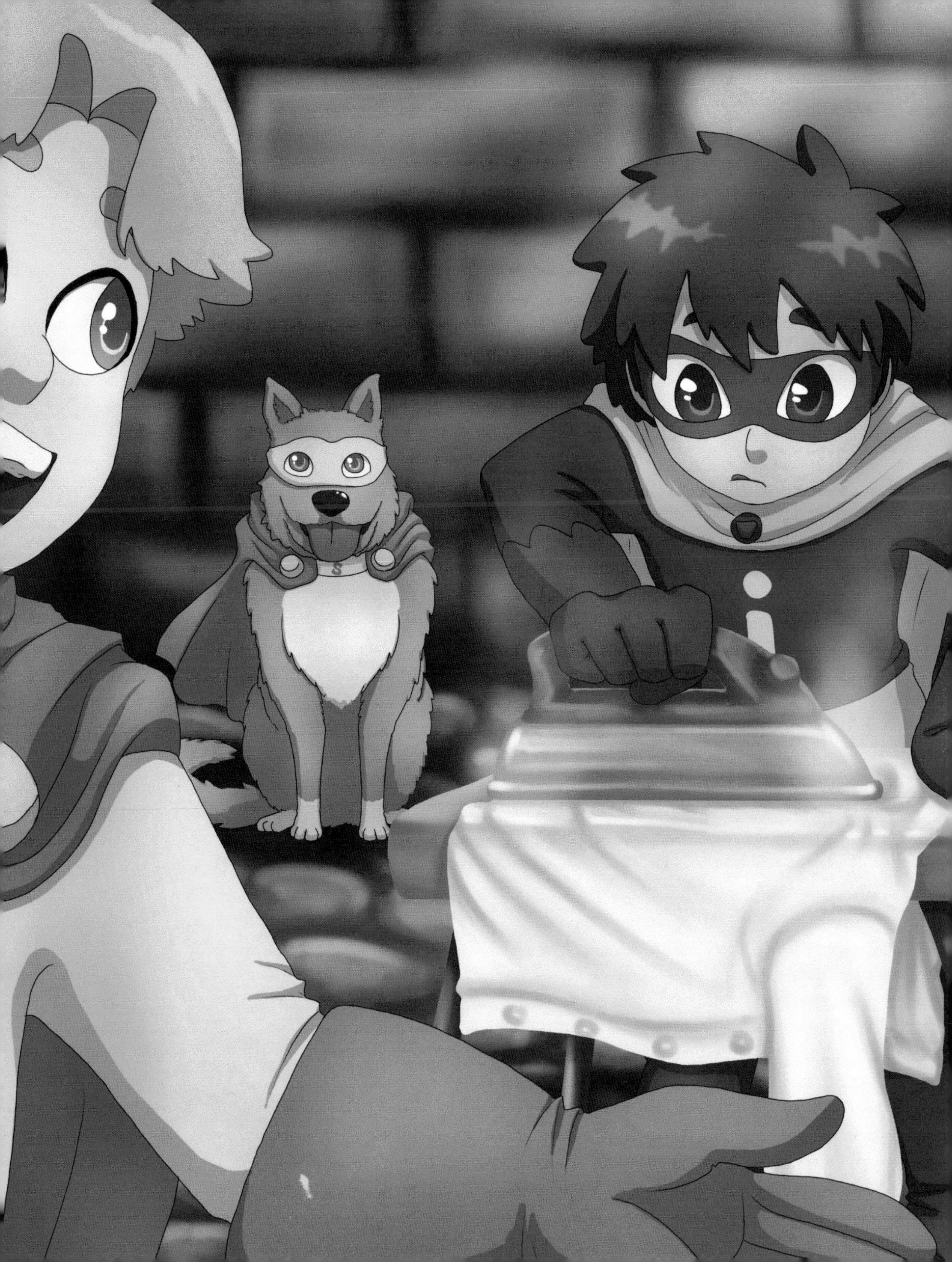

"When selecting a sidekick, it can be a good idea for their name to compliment your own. For example, Eggman and Bacon Boy, The Raincloud and Thunderhead, and Glow Girl and the Shadow Princess all have a nice ring together, don't you think? I dubbed my own sidekick Inferior Dude."

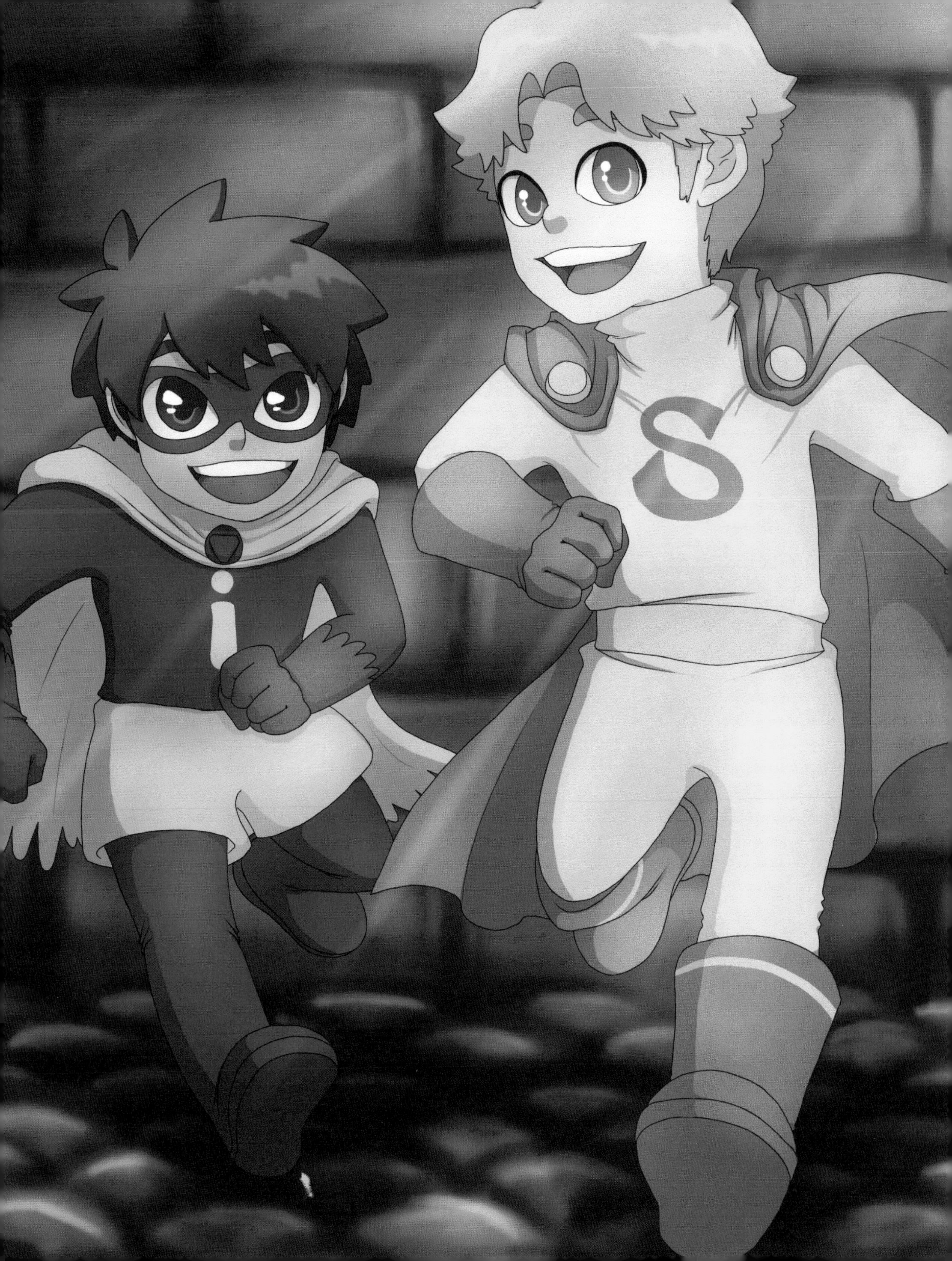

i
S

"It can be tough working solo in the superhero business, even if you have a sidekick. That is when teaming up with fellow superheroes can be handy. There may even come a time when you and a group of other superheroes decide to form an official team. I myself am a founding member of the Liberty Legion. Not only does being part of a group make it easier to win battles, but it also mean that six out of seven times its someone else's turn on dishwashing duty!"

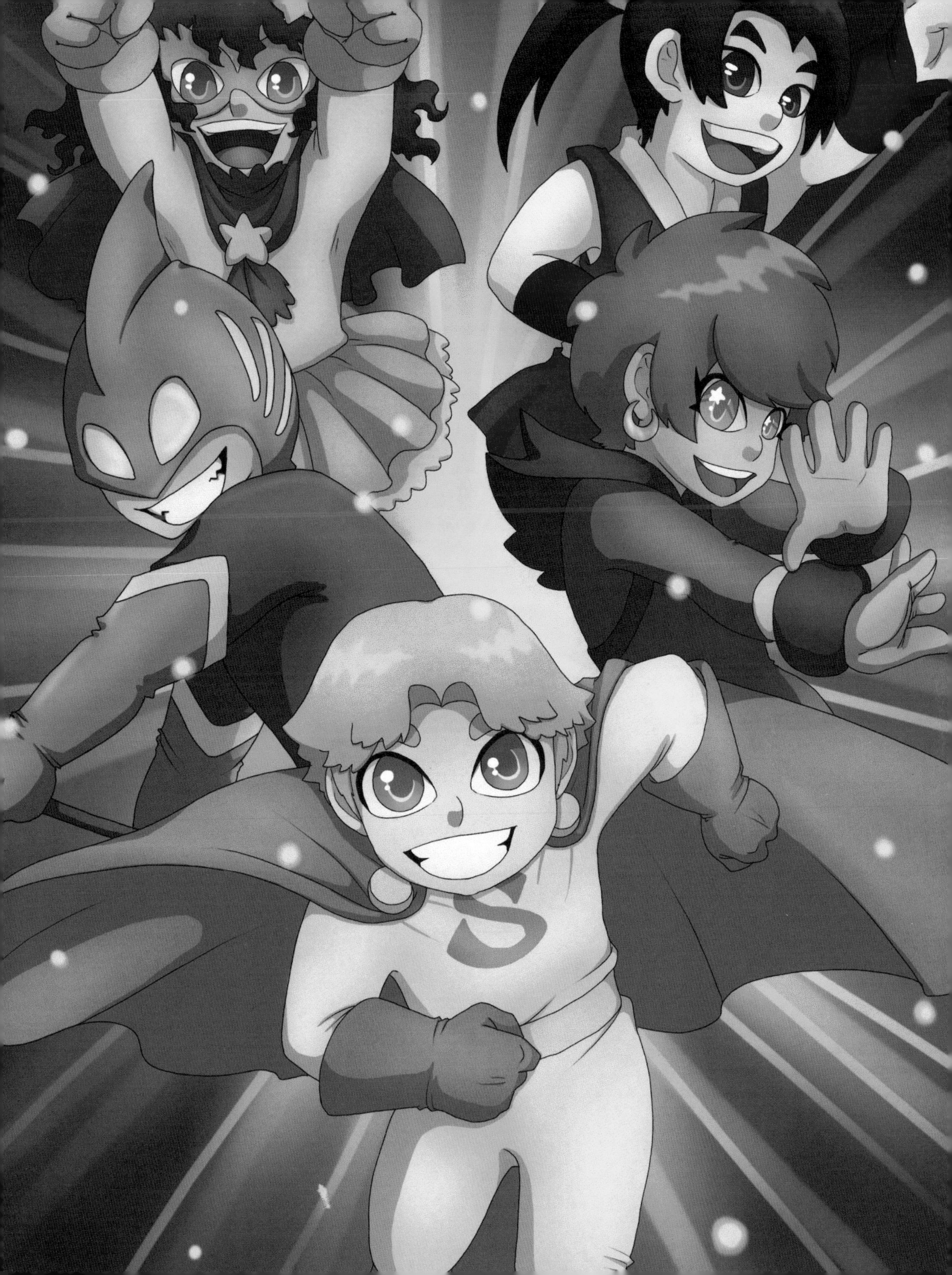

"So, let's see…we've covered posing…secret identities… sidekicks…hmmm, what else should I tell you? Hmm…oh, I know! Follow me.

"As a superhero, I often have to fight in grueling battles. These can be tiring and sometimes just down right frustrating. But, each victory is a shining light, a beacon of hope in the ever crashing sea of good versus evil, and so I like to keep a little trophy from each encounter. After years of superhero work, I've amassed quite a few tokens. Behold, the Superior Trophy Room!"

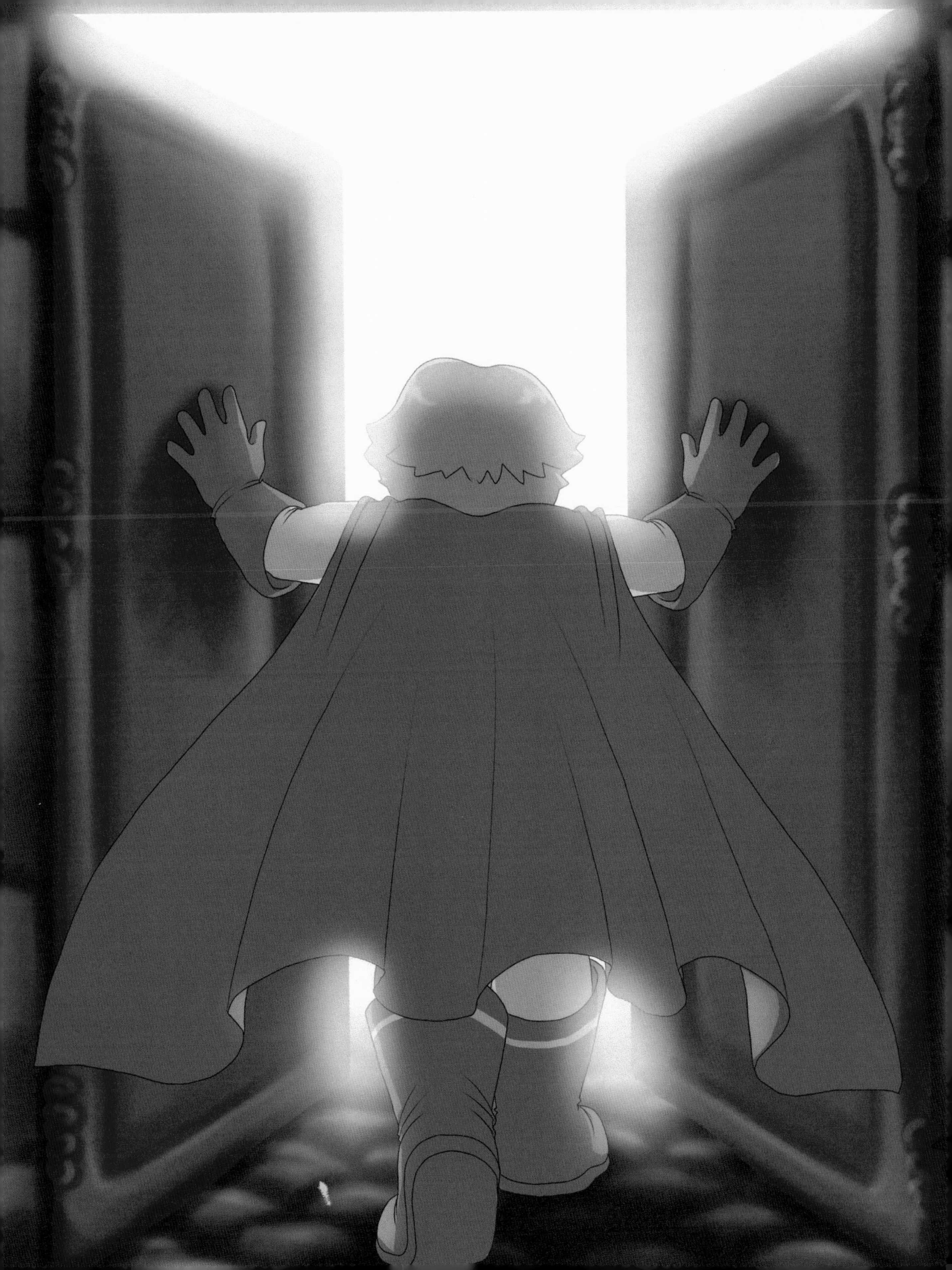

"Here are all the trophies I've collected, each one representing a different crusade against the dark side. Come, look! You're one of the only citizens that have ever seen the Superior Trophy Room!

"This is the unbreakable sword of Merlin's evil twin sister! Over there is the fang of the lizard monster that tried to destroy Japan last month—or was it last week? That is the cranium of the robot that I fought with on the sun—yes, the sun! And this is the magic toaster; it almost wiped out California on New Years. Come this way, please..."

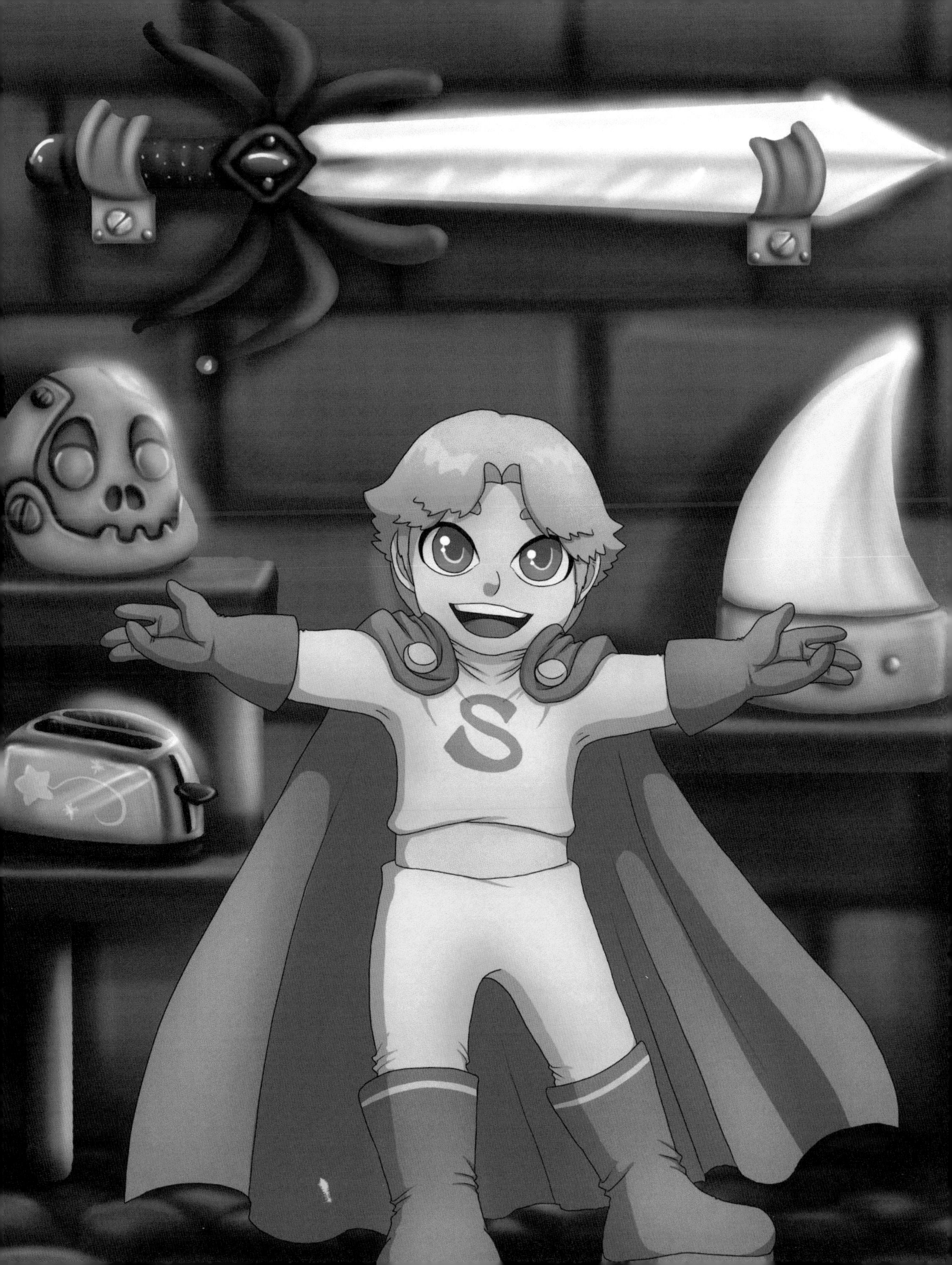

"Here is the giant dime from the bank Benny "Ten" Sence tried to rob last year. There next to it is the toothbrush of Big Bad Boogey Boy, who had surprisingly minty fresh breath. That purple thing in the case is the Bear's squeaky toy. Look—you can see the teeth marks!

"Ah, and this is the licorice stick of Death. Stay away from it! Not only is it incredibly sticky, but if you accidentally eat it, the entire balance of the world will be out of whack! Apocalyptic events will take place! It will be the end of the world!!! Now, moving on..."

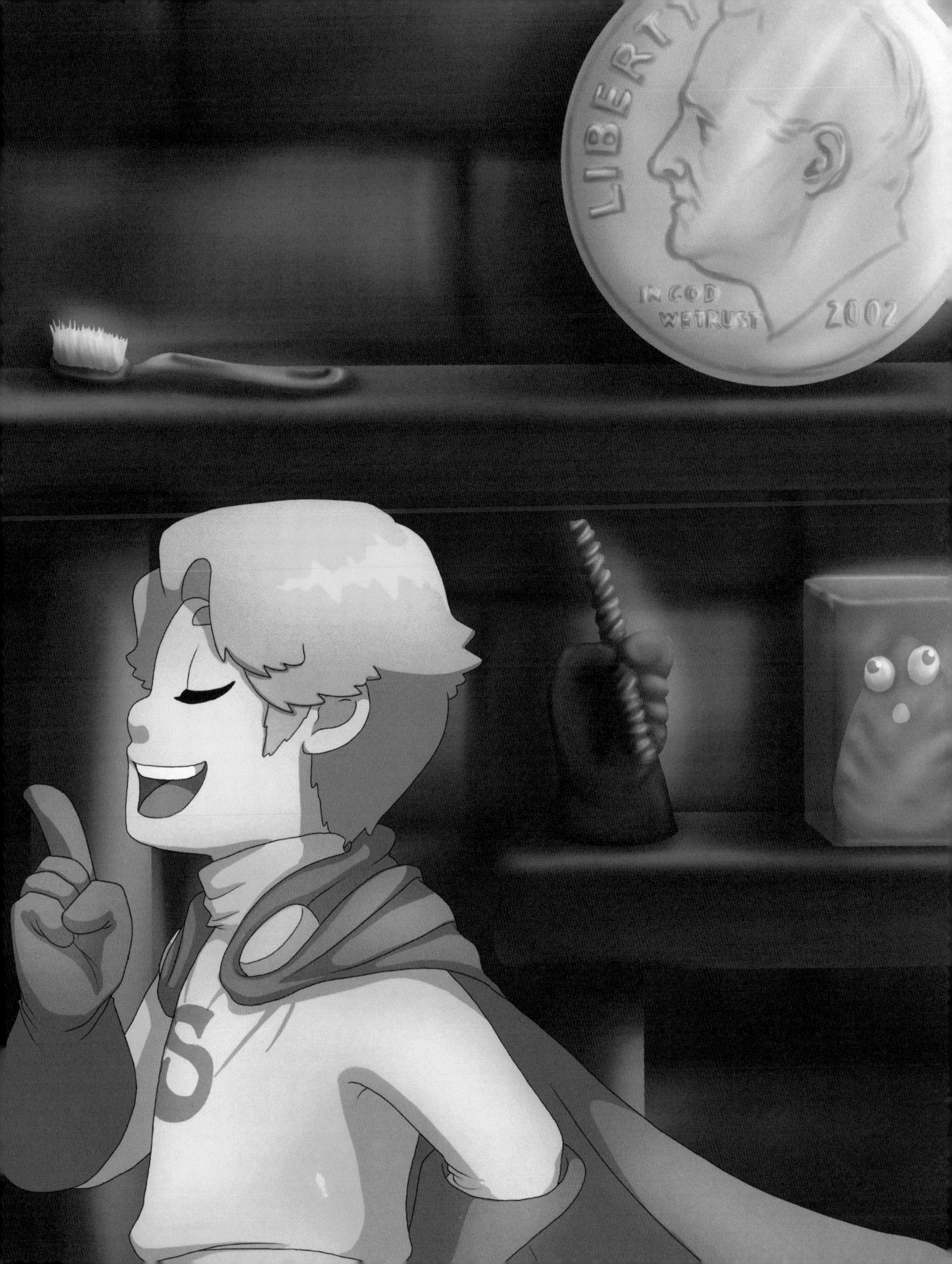
LIBERTY
IN GOD WE TRUST
2002

"In order to have gotten so many trophies, I had to fight many, many evil super villains, and escape many ridiculously complicated death traps involving whoopee cushions, quicksand, Wheels of Doom, and long, horribly clichéd victory speeches! Please follow me into the next room."

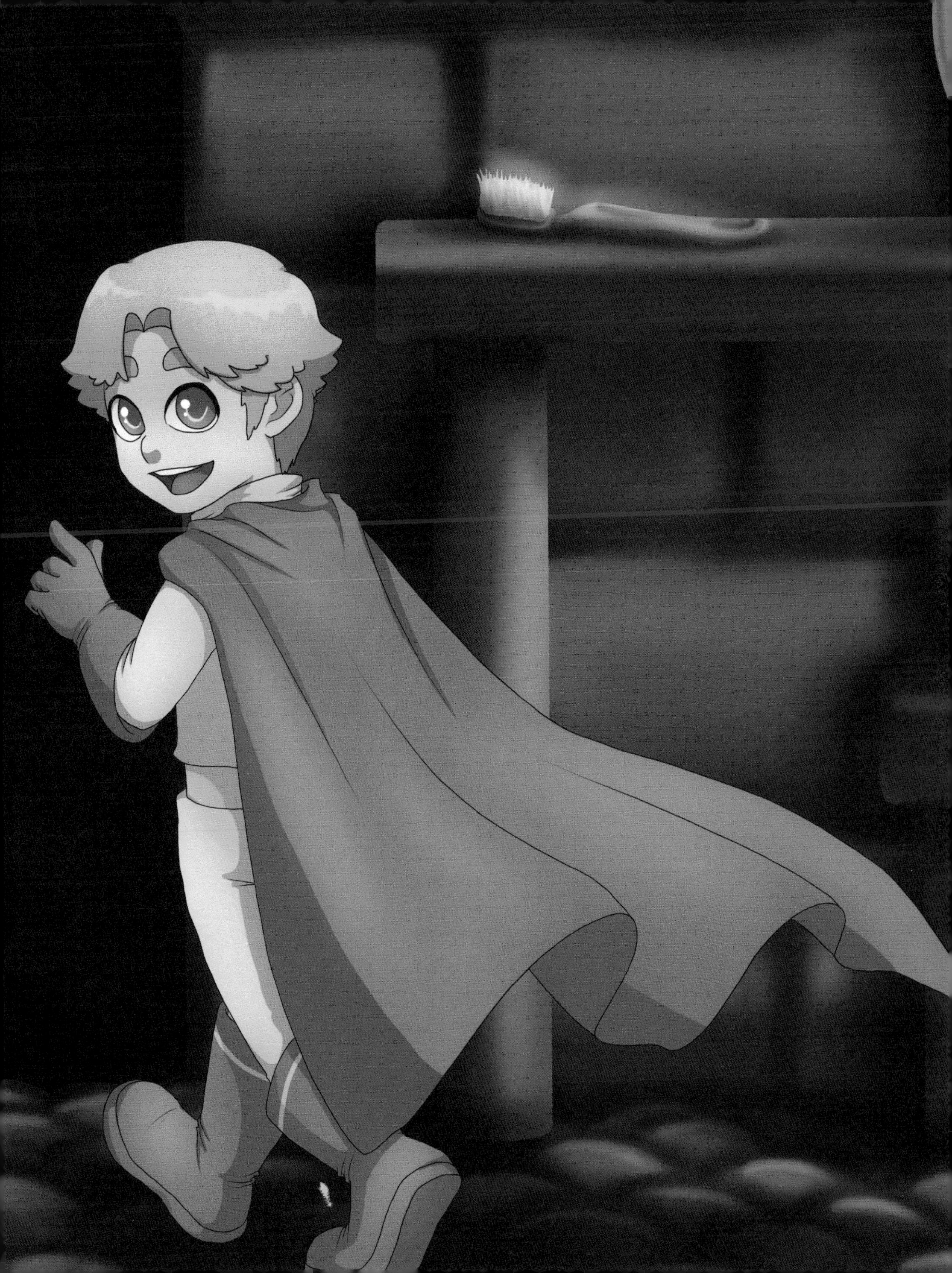

"This—dramatic pause—is Superior Guy's Rogues' Gallery! Here is every dastardly super villain yours truly has ever faced."

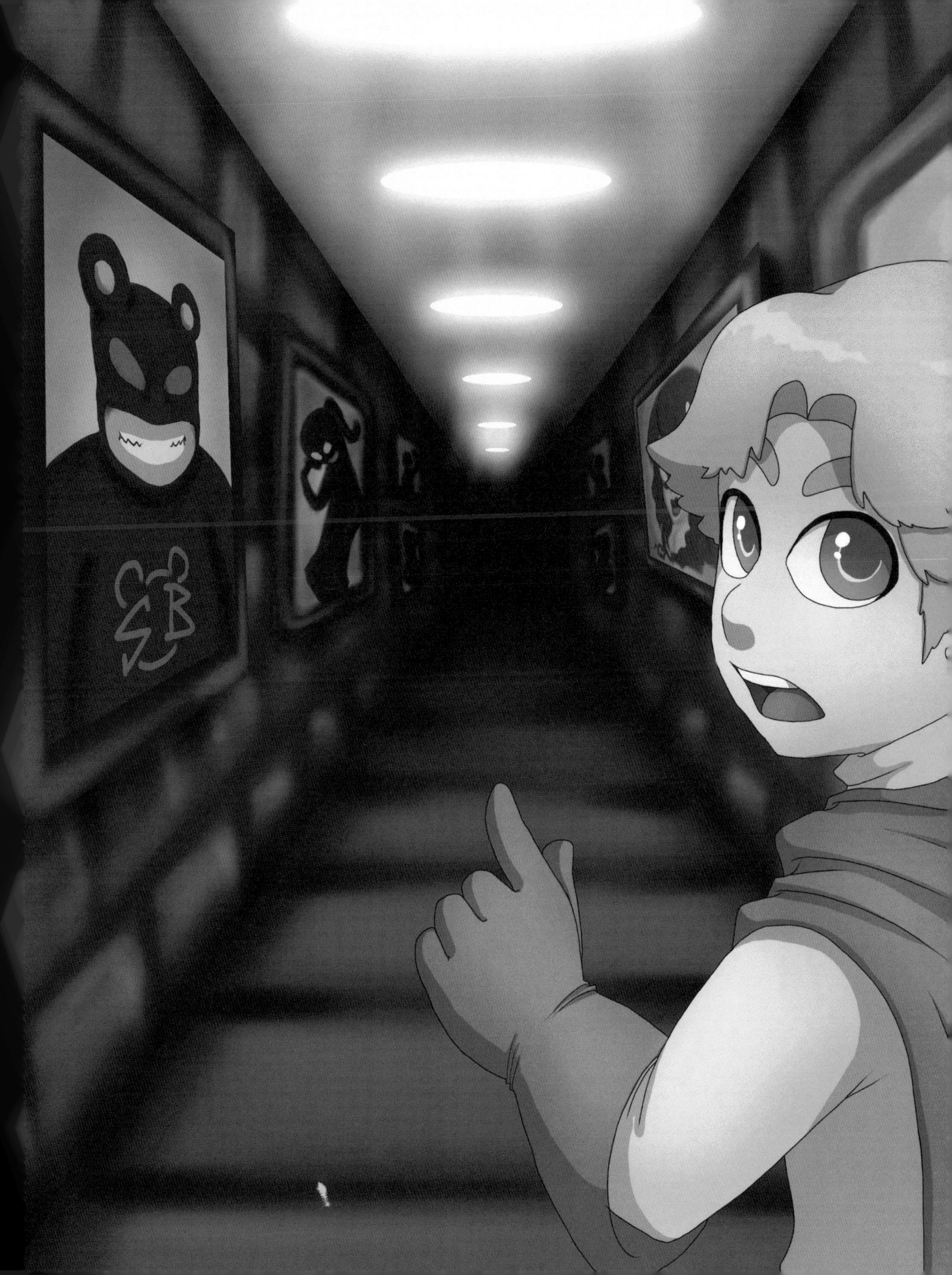

"This is Vegetable Lady, who can control vegetables. She once tried to conquer the world with an army of Brussels sprouts. Next to her is the Fiery Incinerator, who can create fire. Currently he is doing community service at the soup kitchen, where he heats the ovens."

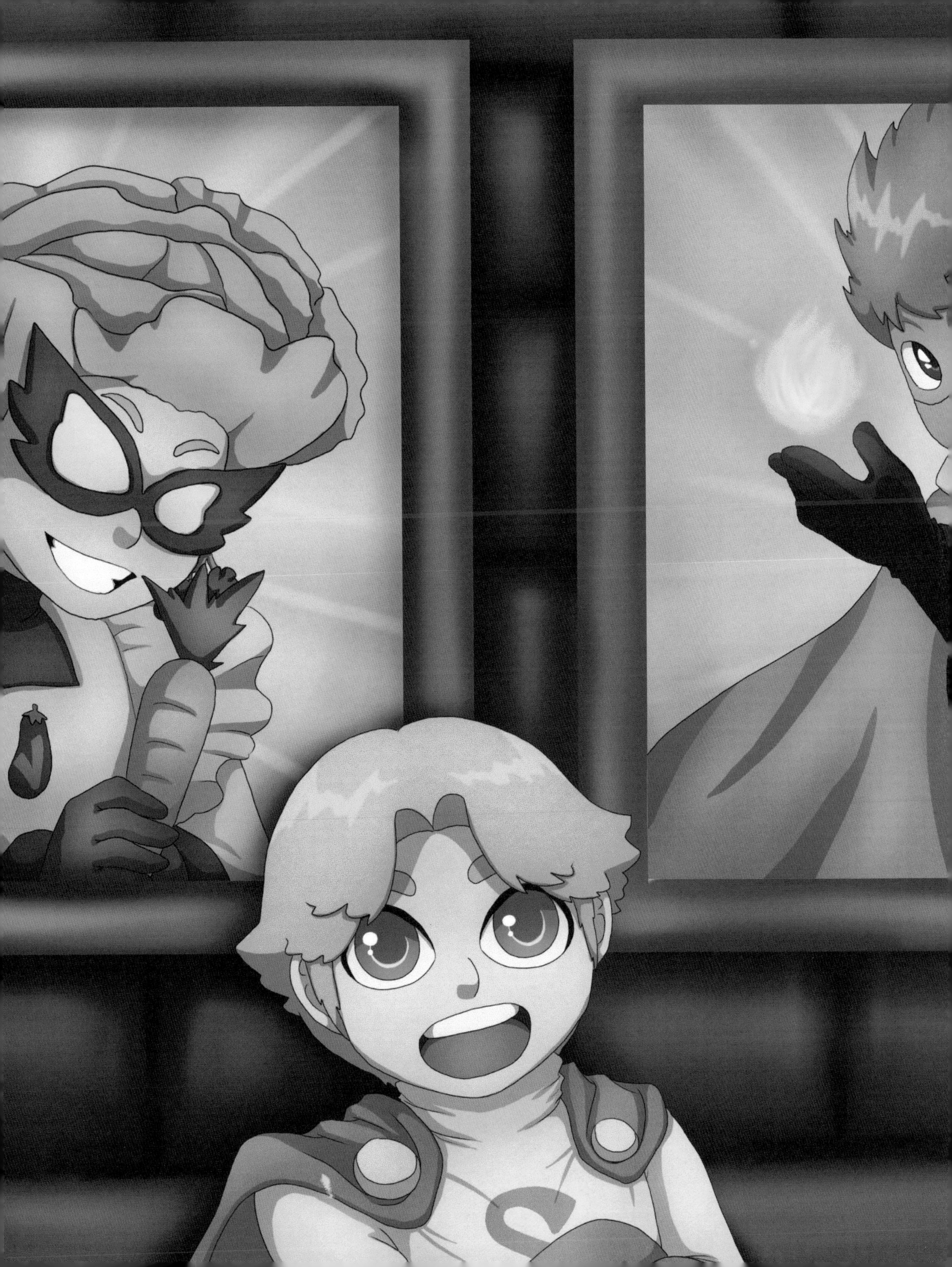

"That is Tom Fool, who once trapped me in a rather complicated death trap involving a conveyor belt, a chain saw, and 50,001 rotten eggs. I, of course, escaped, thanks to my cleverness and the fact that I always start the day with a healthy breakfast! And over there is the Man of Magnets. He once came close to defeating me, but Superior Guy overcomes all challenges! Although I suppose it did help that we were fighting near a home appliance store and he got stuck to a refrigerator."

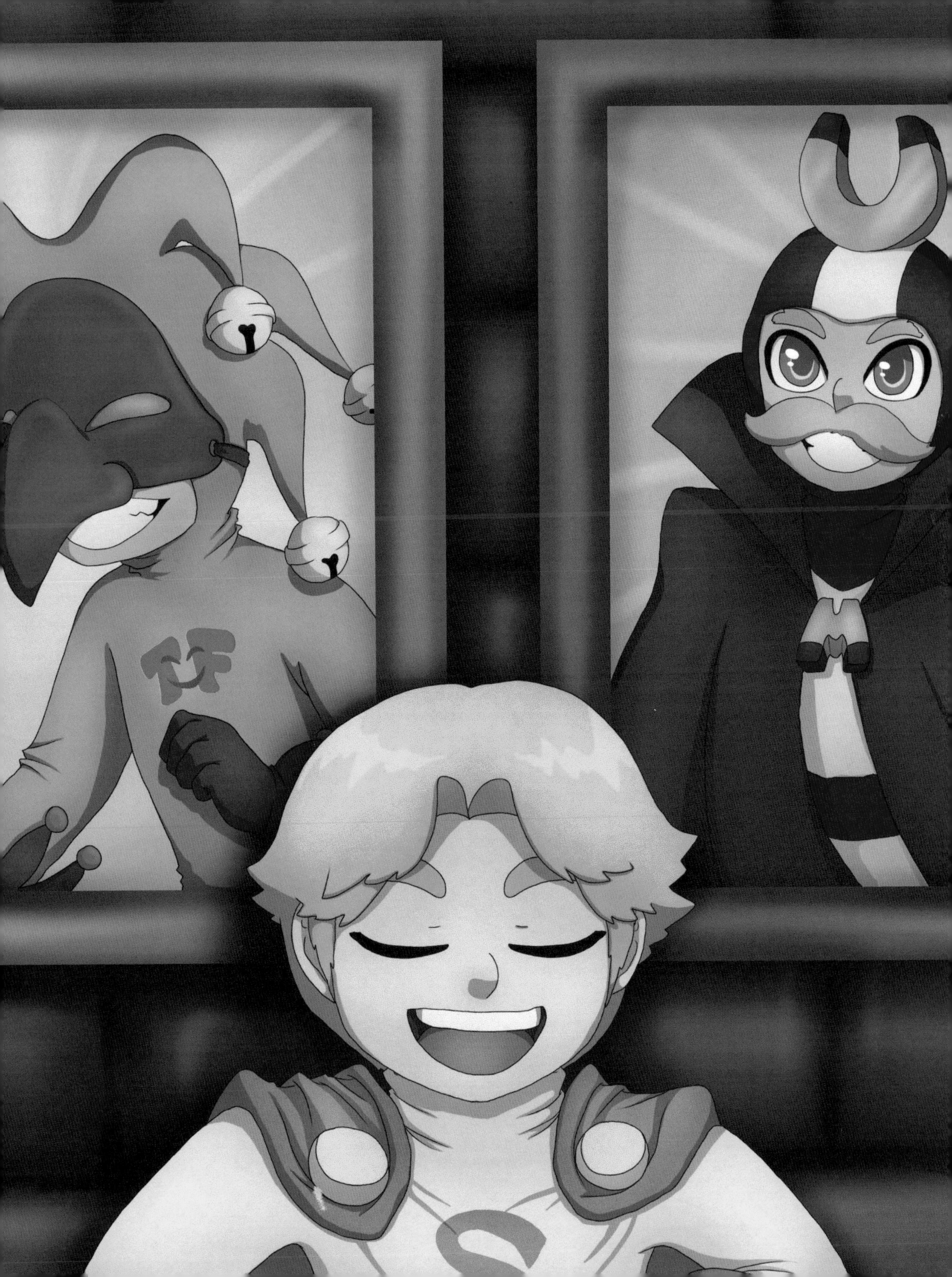

"Ah, here is a very confused young man who calls himself the Supreme Master of Awesomeness. He is more like the Supreme Master of Silliness. He has done some pretty crazy stuff throughout the time I've known him. One time, he tried to turn the moon into cheese! Cheese! Ridiculous!"

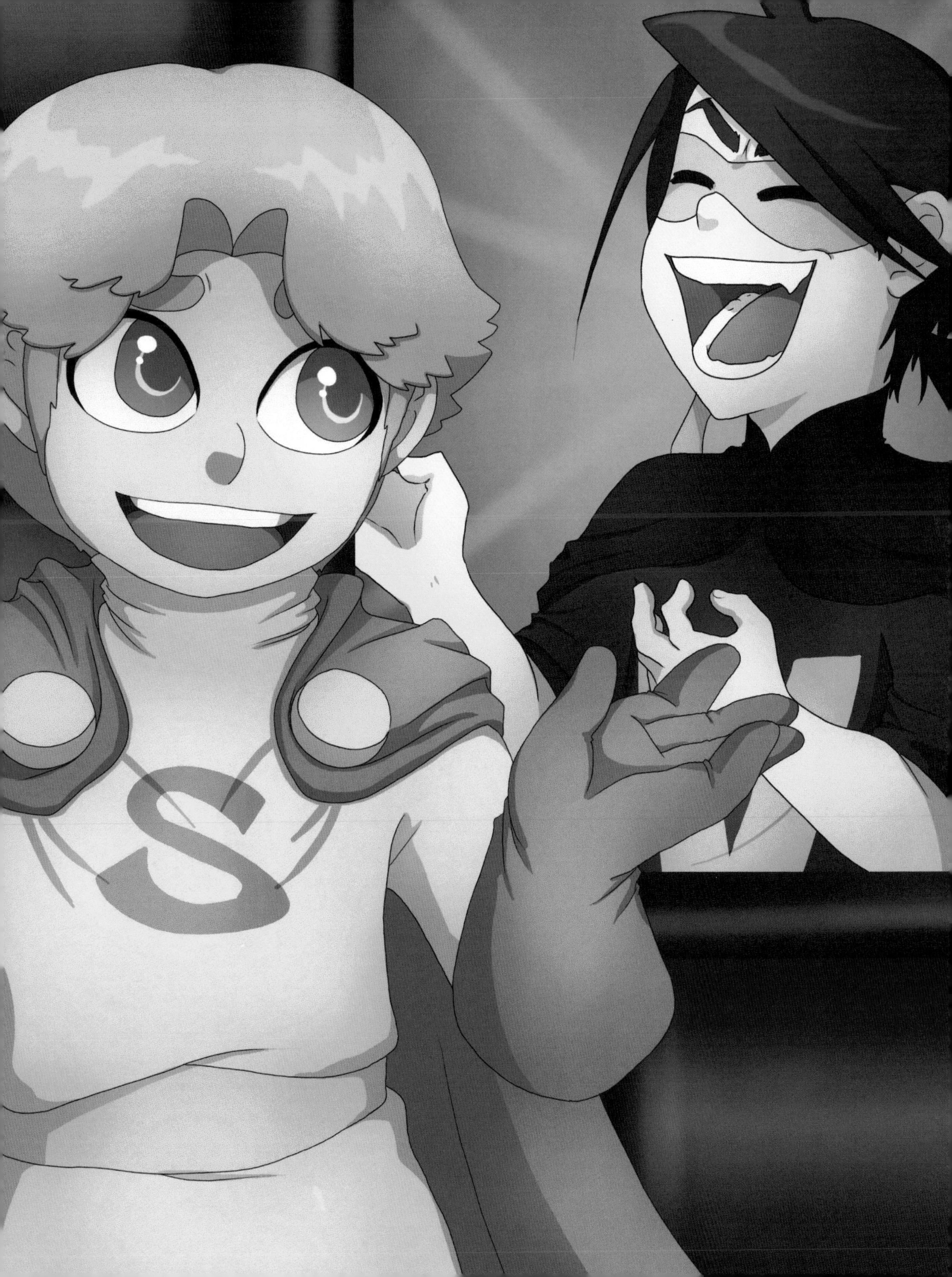

"Now, moving on to Purple Lady, I—"

BEEP! BEEP! BEEP!

"The alarm! Somebody is in trouble! Quick, to the communications room!"

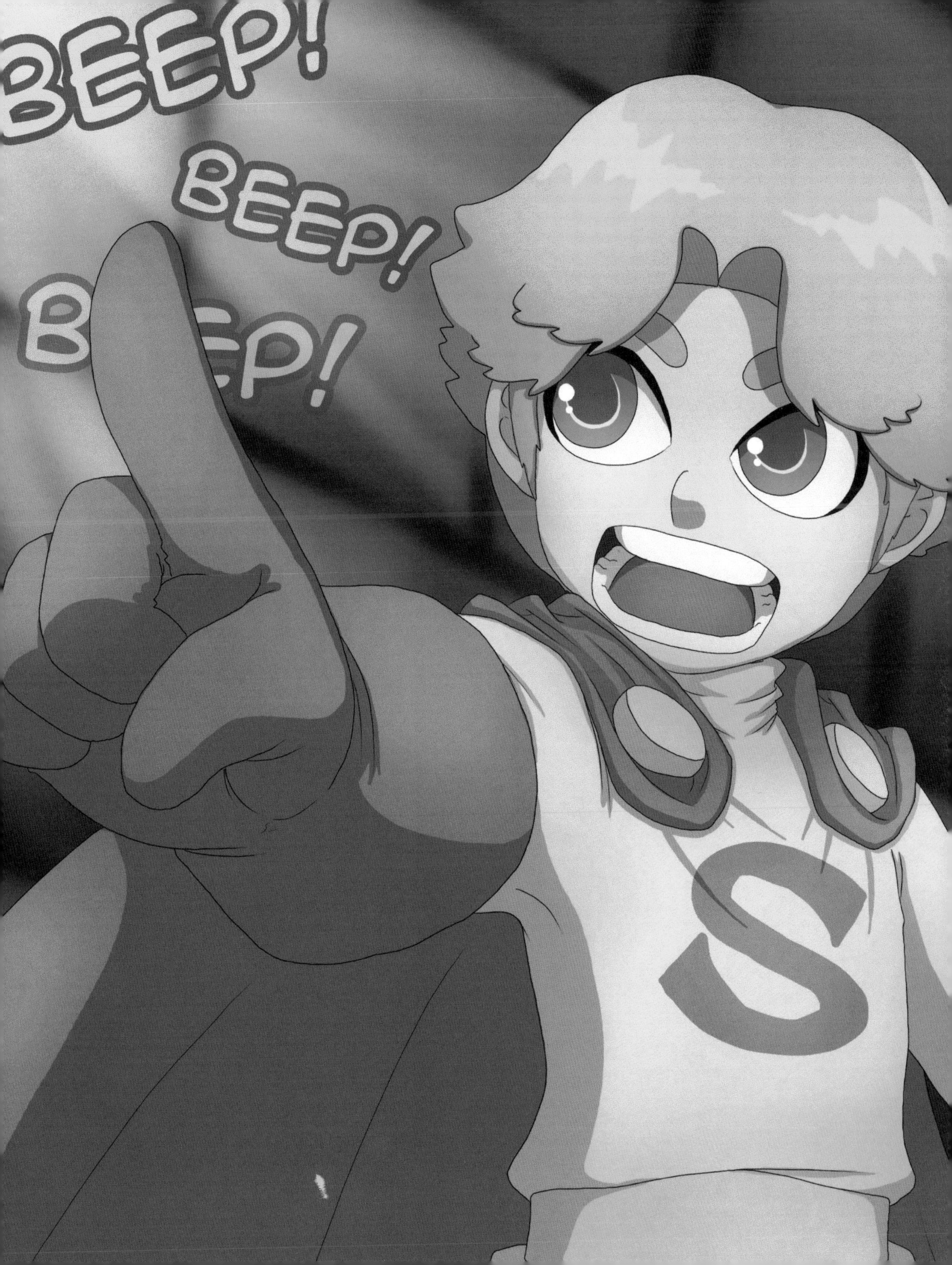
BEEP!
BEEP!
B EP!

"Someone is trying to contact me through the emergency phone line! Please be quiet while I take this call..."

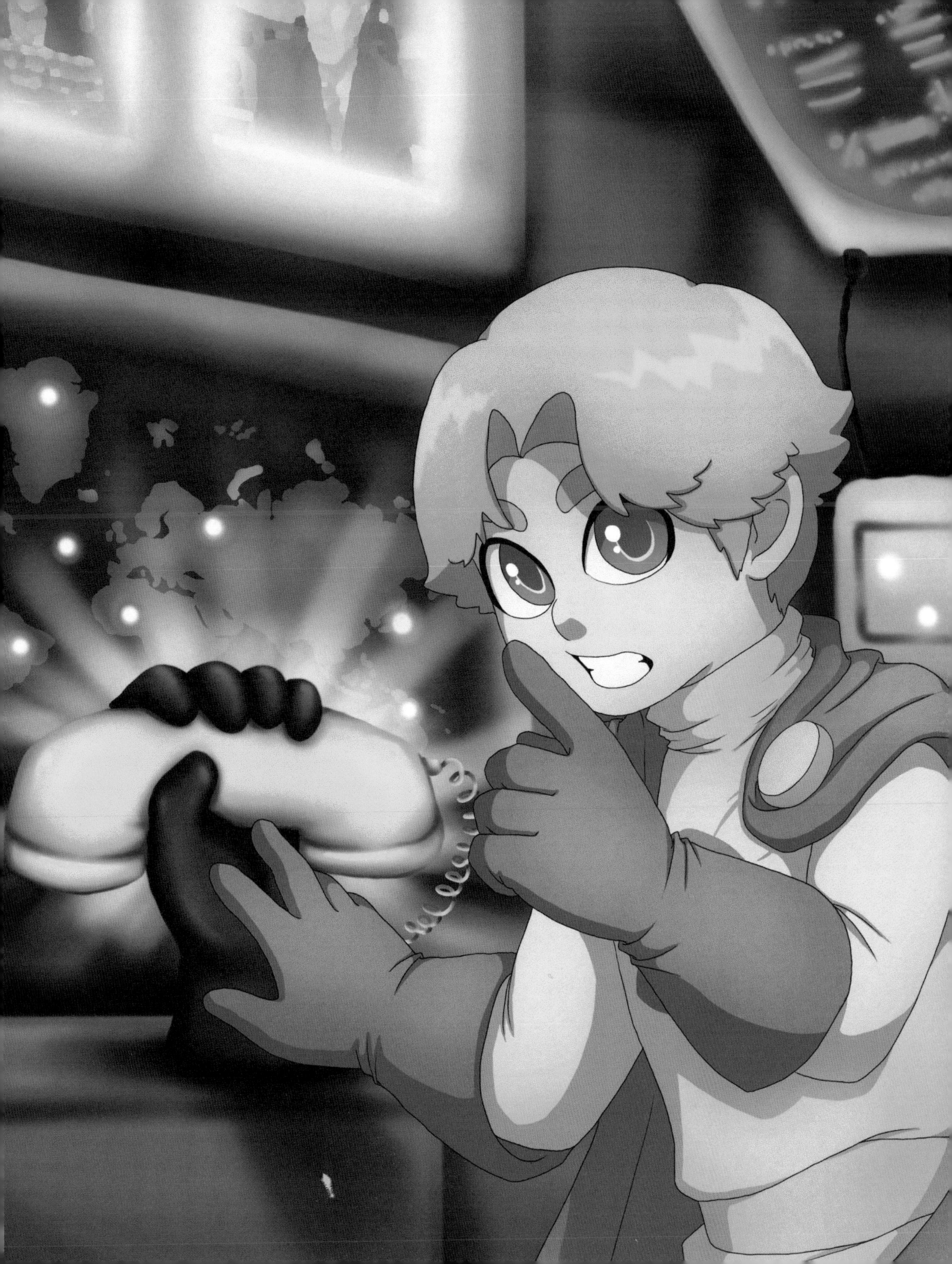

"Hello? Yes...uh huh...really...of course...well, no need to worry, sir! Superior Guy is on the job!"

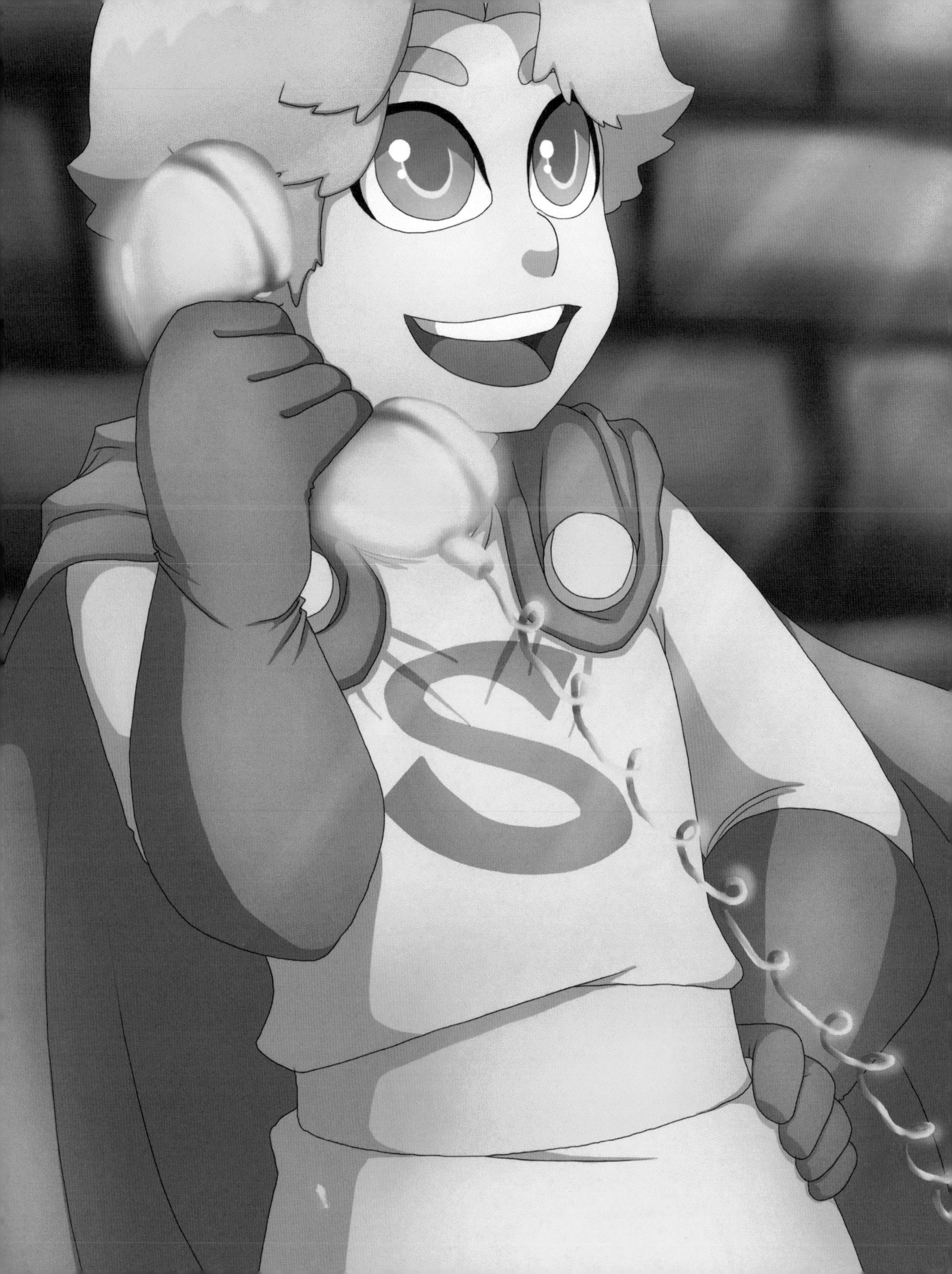

"I must be off, citizen; the city of Super-Duper-Opolis needs a superhero: me! So remember, always brush your teeth, listen to Superior Guy, and never give up the fight against evil! For Liberty, Duty, and Democracy!"

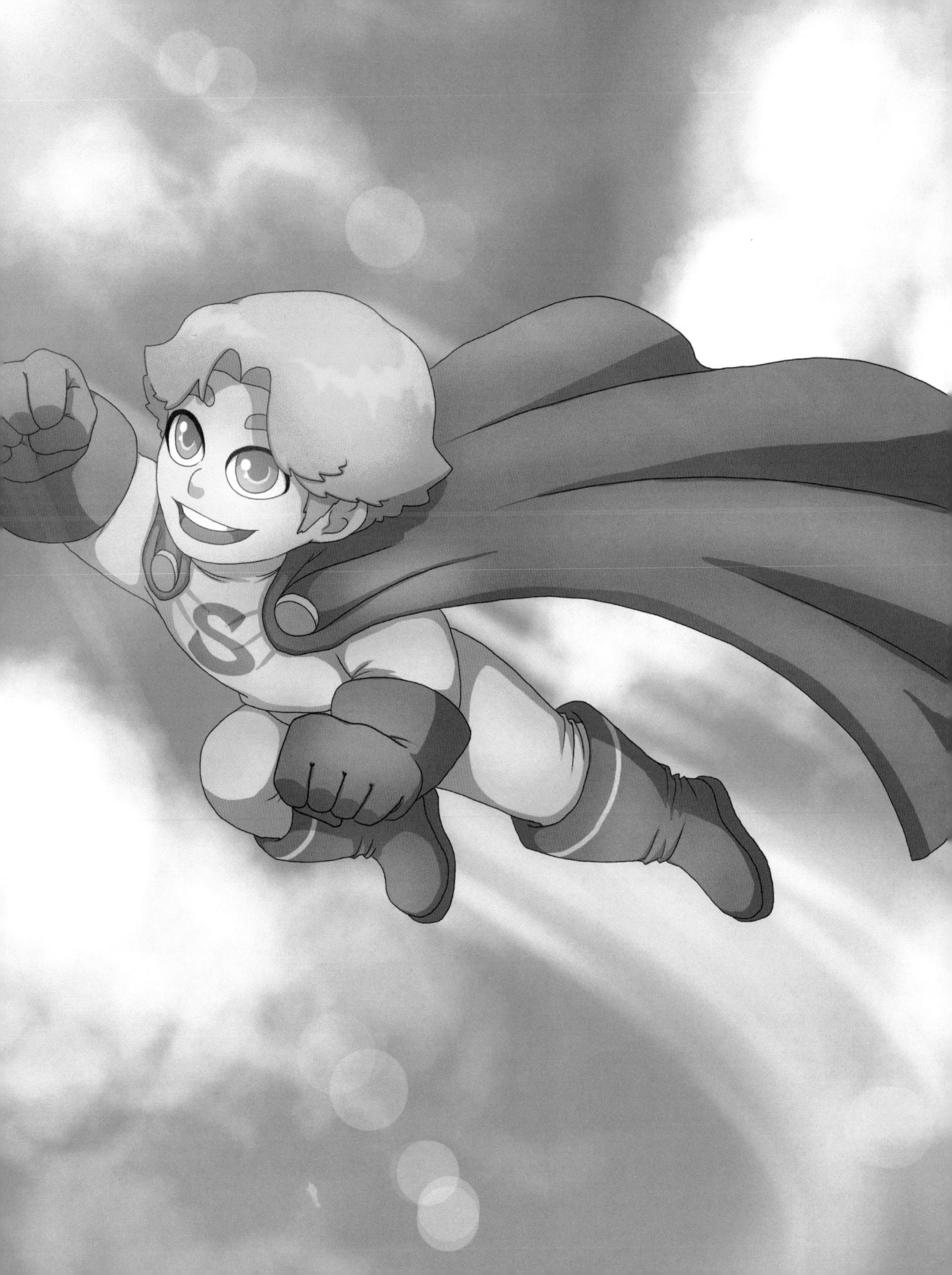
S

Made in the USA
Lexington, KY
09 November 2013